The Cholent Brigade

by **Michael Herman**

Illustrations by **Sharon Harmer**

KAR-BEN
PUBLISHING

On Friday, the day of the big snow, Mr. Monty Nudelman woke up early to shovel.

He shoveled Mrs. Birnbaum's driveway so she wouldn't be late for work.

He cleaned off Mr. Levi's minivan so Mr. Levi
wouldn't be late for carpooling.

And he dug out Rabbi Strauss' car after the snowplow came by and plowed it in.

For hours and hours, Monty Nudelman shoveled. He shoveled walkways, alleyways, steps and stoops. Now his neighbors could walk their dogs, and the mail carrier wouldn't slip and fall.

Thanks to Monty, kids could catch the school bus, and parents could run their errands and shop for Shabbat.

With one last heave of his shovel, Monty cleared off the snow from the fire hydrant in front of his house, and . . .

"YEOWW!"

A fiery pain shot through Monty Nudelman's back.

It hurt so much that he could barely hobble inside.

The next day, at Shabbat services, everyone at the synagogue asked,
"Where is Monty Nudelman?"

"He hurt his back when he was out shoveling," came the answer.

The congregation said the special get-well prayer for him.

Back at home, before the Birnbaum family sat down to their Shabbat lunch, Mrs. Birnbaum handed her son, Izzy, a large foil-covered bowl. "This bowl is filled with warmth and comfort," she told him. "Please take it to Monty. There is nothing like a tasty cholent to make someone feel better."

Armed with the bowl of cholent, Izzy headed
out the door to Monty Nudelman's house.

Over at the Levi house, Mr. Levi had just finished setting the table for Shabbat lunch. He handed his daughter, Mirra, a small covered pot. "This pot is filled with happiness," he said. "Please take it to Monty."

At the Strauss house the rabbi called to the twins. He handed Sophie and Sam a large thermos. "This thermos is filled with friendship," he told them. "Please take it to Monty."

When the twins stepped outside, they saw their friend Hannah.
She was carrying something too.

"Where are you going?" asked Sophie.

"To Monty Nudelman's house."

Along the way, they met Mirra carrying her pot, and
Izzy with his bowl.

As they turned the corner, they saw Nathan and Benji, Emma and Abby, Lila, Jonah, and Jack. All heading to Monty Nudelman's house.

It was a cholent brigade!

Monty Nudelman was sitting at the window, feeling lonely, when he saw a parade of boys and girls marching through the snow.

"Where are they going?" he wondered.

The brigade trudged up Monty's snow-packed sidewalk, and Sophie knocked on the door.

"I'm coming," Monty answered.

They waited.

And waited.

"Still coming," he called.

When the door finally opened, there was Monty Nudelman, all hunched over.

"Shabbat shalom, Monty!" everyone cried. **"We brought you cholent!"**

"What a surprise!" exclaimed Monty.

The cholent brigade marched inside and set their bowls and pots and containers on Monty's dining room table.

"There's enough here to feed an army," said Monty. "I hope you can stay and help me eat this."

Monty eased himself into a chair, and everyone sat down around him.

They ate cholent with beef and potatoes, beans and barley. They ate cholent with chicken and carrots and mushrooms, cholent with short ribs and sweet potatoes, and even chili cholent. Each dish was filled with warmth and comfort, happiness and friendship.

"This is a true feast," said Monty. "And the best part is sharing it with you."

On Sunday, the cholent brigade returned to Monty Nudelman's house.

This time to shovel his sidewalk.

Cholent recipe

Cholent is a traditional Jewish stew that dates back many centuries. It is prepared on Friday before sundown, cooks through the night, and is eaten for Shabbat lunch. There are many recipes for cholent. Here is a classic one—with the addition of carrots and barbecue sauce.

Ingredients

- 1 cup (200 g) mixed dried beans (kidney, navy, pinto, lima)
- 1 cup (200 g) barley
- 2 medium onions, chopped
- 4-6 cloves garlic, chopped
- 12 small red potatoes, quartered
- ½ pound (227 g) baby carrots
- 3 pounds (1,361 g) stew meat, cubed
- ¼ cup (6 mL) oil
- 2 tsp. (6 g) salt
- ½ tsp. (3 g) pepper
- ½ cup (120 mL) barbecue sauce

Preparation

Soak the beans overnight. Drain and rinse.

In a 6-quart (6L) slow cooker, pour in the oil. Add the onions, garlic, potatoes, carrots, beans, barley, and meat. Sprinkle in the salt and pepper, and top with barbecue sauce. Fill with water until just barely covered. Set cooker to low and let cook through the night into late morning.

Serves 10

Remembering my grandmother, Leah Baran, who filled each dish with love. —M.H.

For Mum & Dad, for all their support —S.H.

Michael Herman has a passion for Jewish history and tradition, and enjoys collecting antique Judaica. Every Friday before Shabbat, he prepares cholent in his grandmother's antique cholent pot. Michael lives in Chicago, Illinois. He is also the author of *Under The Sabbath Lamp.*

Sharon Harmer lives and works on the south coast of England, and has illustrated many children's books. She especially enjoys creating characters, and her illustrations are a mixture of traditional and digital, incorporating hand-drawn line and painted textures. A background in botany and love of nature and travel also inform her work.

KAR-BEN PUBLISHING, INC.
A division of Lerner Publishing Group, Inc.
241 First Avenue North
Minneapolis, MN 55401 USA
1-800-4-KARBEN
Website address: www.karben.com

Library of Congress Cataloging-in-Publication Data

Names: Herman, Michael, 1964- author. | Harmer, Sharon, illustrator.
Title: The cholent brigade / by Michael Herman ; illustrated by Sharon Harmer.
Description: Minneapolis : Kar-Ben Publishing, [2017] | Summary: When Monty Nudelman throws his back out shoveling neighborhood sidewalks and driveways, his neighbors help him in return by sending their children with hot bowls of stew for his Shabbat lunch.
Identifiers: LCCN 2016028083| ISBN 9781512408447 (lb : alk. paper) | ISBN 9781512408454 (pb : alk. paper)
Subjects: | CYAC: Neighborliness—Fiction. | Jews—United States—Fiction. | Sabbath—Fiction.
Classification: LCC PZ7.1.H494 Cho 2017 | DDC [E]—dc23

LC record available at https://lccn.loc.gov/2016028083

Manufactured in the United States of America
1-39402-21216-9/7/2016